SAN ANTONIO SPURS

ALL-TIME GREATS

BY BRENDAN FLYNN

Book design by Jake Slavik
Cover design by Jake Slavik

Photographs ©: Eric Gay/AP Images, cover (top), 1 (top); Jeff Roberson/AP Images, cover (bottom), 1 (bottom); Focus on Sport/Getty Images Sport/Getty Images, 4, 7; Focus on Sport/Getty Images Sport Classic/Getty Images 8; Phil Huber/Sports Illustrated/Set Number: X40541 TK1 R2 F8/Getty Images, 10; John Biever/Sports Illustrated/Set Number: X73686 TK1/Getty Images, 13; Greg Nelson/Sports Illustrated/Set Number: X74749 TK1/Getty Images, 14; Bob Rosato/Sports Illustrated/Set Number: X78261 TK1 R17/Getty Images, 16; Brandon Wade/Fort Worth Star-Telegram/Tribune News Service/Getty Images, 18; Ronald Cortes/Getty Images Sport/Getty Images, 20; Aaron Ontiveroz/MediaNews Group/The Denver Post/Getty Images, 21; Red Line Editorial, 22

Press Box Books, an imprint of Press Room Editions.

ISBN
978-1-63494-160-0 (library bound)
978-1-63494-173-0 (paperback)
978-1-63494-186-0 (epub)
978-1-63494-199-0 (hosted ebook)

Library of Congress Control Number: 2019951067

Distributed by North Star Editions, Inc.
2297 Waters Drive
Mendota Heights, MN 55120
www.northstareditions.com

Printed in the United States of America
012020

ABOUT THE AUTHOR

Brendan Flynn is a San Francisco resident and an author of numerous children's books. In addition to writing about sports, Flynn also enjoys competing in triathlons, Scrabble tournaments, and chili cook-offs.

TABLE OF CONTENTS

GERVIN
44

CHAPTER 1
PIONEERS

The San Antonio Spurs didn't always play in San Antonio or even in the NBA. The Spurs are one of four current NBA teams that began in the American Basketball Association (ABA). They were formed in 1967 as the Dallas Chaparrals. In 1973 they moved to their current home, and they joined the NBA in 1976.

One of their earliest stars was **George Gervin**. The silky swingman was one of the greatest scorers of all time. He led the NBA in scoring four times. His career average of 25.1 points per game ranks 10th in NBA history.

Nicknamed "the Iceman," Gervin was the coolest player on the court. He was famous for ending a drive to the hoop with a delicate finger roll layup. He was also a threat to score from anywhere inside of 30 feet.

> **GREAT GERVIN**
> Only two players have won more NBA scoring titles than Gervin did. Michael Jordan led the league in scoring 10 times. Wilt Chamberlain won seven scoring titles.

James Silas was Gervin's longtime backcourt mate in San Antonio. Silas was a clutch scorer who made big shots in important moments. He was an ABA All-Star two straight years, but injuries caused him to miss most of the next two seasons.

Silas came back and played at a high level for three more years as the Spurs established

SILAS
13

GILMORE
53

themselves in the NBA. They made the playoffs in each of their first seven NBA seasons. In 1982–83 they fell two wins short of reaching the NBA Finals. One of the stars of that team was center **Artis Gilmore**.

The 7'2" Gilmore was a presence in the middle. If he got the ball near the basket, he was almost impossible to stop. He used power moves and a polished hook shot to lead the league in field goal percentage six times, including twice in his five seasons as a Spur.

STAT SPOTLIGHT

SINGLE-SEASON POINTS PER GAME

SPURS TEAM RECORD

George Gervin: 33.1 (1979-80)

ROBINSON

50

CHAPTER 2

CHAMPIONS

The Spurs eventually put together a dynasty. They won five NBA titles between 1999 and 2014. But the first steps toward greatness were taken in 1989 when **David Robinson** arrived on the scene. The 7'1" center was named NBA Rookie of the Year. He averaged 24.3 points, 12.0 rebounds, and 3.9 blocked shots per game in 1989–90.

And Robinson got better from there. He was the NBA Most Valuable Player (MVP) in 1995. The 10-time All-Star was also an excellent passer and ran the floor well for a big man.

But Robinson couldn't do it alone. Help arrived when the Spurs landed **Tim Duncan** with the first pick of the 1997 draft. The Spurs had the first pick because Robinson was injured in 1996–97. He missed all but six games that season, and they finished 20–62.

SALUTE!

Robinson attended the US Naval Academy. He had to serve in the Navy for two years before he could join the Spurs. Once he reached the NBA, he picked up a nautical nickname– "The Admiral."

Like Robinson, Duncan won the NBA Rookie of the Year Award. The next season, he was the MVP of the NBA Finals as the Spurs won

STAT SPOTLIGHT

CAREER GAMES PLAYED

SPURS TEAM RECORD

Tim Duncan: 1,392

DUNCAN
21

COACH
POPOVICH
PARKER
9
PARKER
9

their first NBA title. The 6'11" Duncan teamed with Robinson to dominate opponents near the basket. His low-post moves on offense and shot blocking on defense helped him make the All-Star team 15 times.

Duncan was the Finals MVP two more times and was also a two-time regular-season MVP. He and head coach **Gregg Popovich** were part of all five Spurs championship teams. Two other players won four rings in San Antonio. Both were products of the Spurs' international scouting.

Point guard **Tony Parker** grew up in France and didn't play college basketball. The Spurs took him with the 28th pick in the 2001 NBA Draft. He turned out to be a steal. Parker was a six-time All-Star and was the MVP of the

2007 NBA Finals. Parker spent 17 seasons in San Antonio.

Duncan, Parker, and **Manu Ginóbili** were called "the Big Three." They were the team's biggest stars after Robinson retired in 2003. The Spurs won at least 50 games in 18 consecutive seasons. The Big Three were a big part of most of those teams.

Ginóbili was a player who did a lot of things well. A second-round pick from Argentina, he came off the bench in more than half of his career games. But in his 16 seasons with the Spurs, he became a fan favorite as he gave the team whatever it seemed to need in every game.

CONTRIBUTORS

Forward **Sean Elliott** played 11 of his 12 NBA seasons with the Spurs. He was a starter on the 1998–99 championship team. Two years later, NBA journeyman **Bruce Bowen** signed with the Spurs at age 30. His defensive play at forward helped San Antonio win three more NBA titles.

LEONARD
2

CHAPTER 3

MODERN STARS

After a six-year drought, the Spurs won their fifth NBA title in 2014. That year, the Big Three were still together. But the MVP of the Finals was third-year forward **Kawhi Leonard**. He was a relative unknown at the time—not a big scorer or rebounder. Leonard played tenacious defense, however.

His offensive game was rounding into shape too. In the Finals against the Miami Heat, Leonard scored 71 points over the last three games. He led the team in scoring in each of those games, and the Spurs won all three to clinch the title.

After spending nine years with the Portland Trail Blazers, Texas native **LaMarcus Aldridge** came home to play for the Spurs in 2015. The burly center averaged 20 points per game over his first four seasons as a Spur. He also made the

All-Star team three times.

Meanwhile, in 2018 Leonard was traded to Toronto, where he won his second NBA title. In return, the Spurs got guard **DeMar DeRozan**.

DeRozan didn't miss a beat. He averaged more than 20 points per game for the sixth straight season. He also gave the Spurs another All-Star talent to build around as the team looks for its next title.

TIMELINE

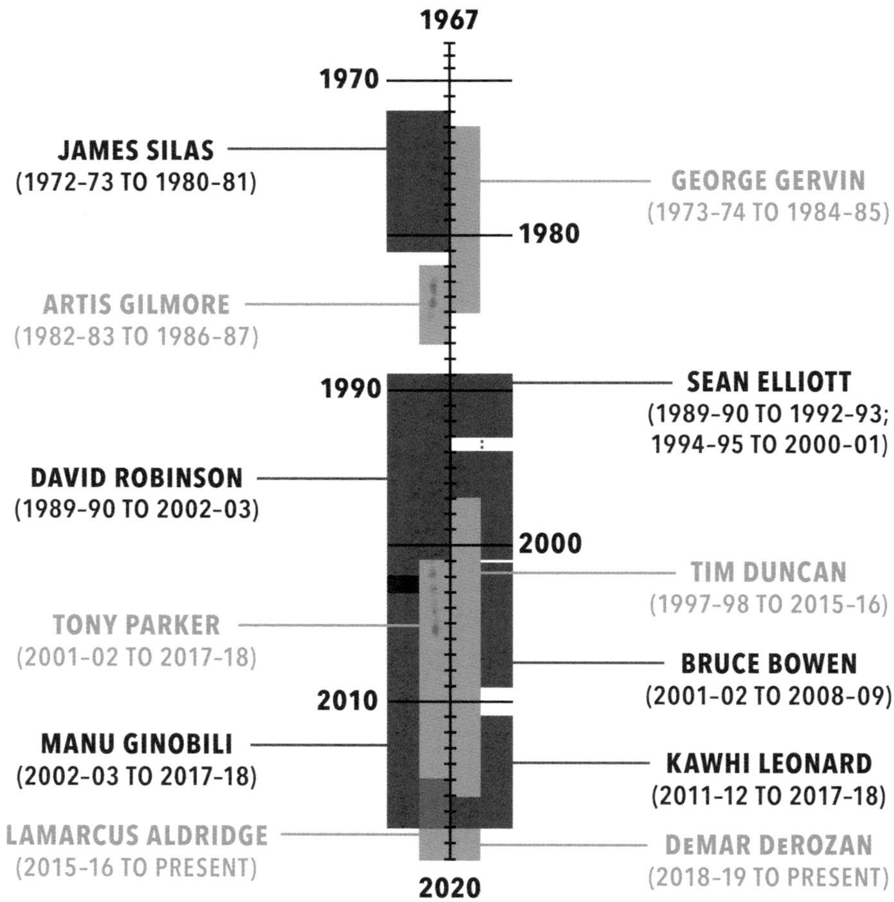
1967
1970
JAMES SILAS
(1972-73 TO 1980-81)
GEORGE GERVIN
(1973-74 TO 1984-85)
1980
ARTIS GILMORE
(1982-83 TO 1986-87)
1990
SEAN ELLIOTT
(1989-90 TO 1992-93; 1994-95 TO 2000-01)
DAVID ROBINSON
(1989-90 TO 2002-03)
2000
TIM DUNCAN
(1997-98 TO 2015-16)
TONY PARKER
(2001-02 TO 2017-18)
BRUCE BOWEN
(2001-02 TO 2008-09)
2010
MANU GINOBILI
(2002-03 TO 2017-18)
KAWHI LEONARD
(2011-12 TO 2017-18)
LAMARCUS ALDRIDGE
(2015-16 TO PRESENT)
DEMAR DEROZAN
(2018-19 TO PRESENT)
2020

TEAM FACTS

SAN ANTONIO SPURS

Formerly: Dallas Chaparrals (1967–68 to 1972–73)

First season: 1967–68

NBA championships: 5*

Key coaches:

Stan Albeck (1980–81 to 1982–83)
153–93, 13–14 playoffs

Doug Moe (1976–77 to 1979–80)
177–135, 9–13 playoffs

Gregg Popovich (1996–97 to present)
1245–575, 170–114 playoffs, 5 NBA titles

MORE INFORMATION

To learn more about the San Antonio Spurs, go to **pressboxbooks.com/AllAccess.**

These links are routinely monitored and updated to provide the most current information available.

**Through 2018–19 season*

GLOSSARY

burly
Large and strong; powerfully built.

clutch
Able to come through in important or pressure-packed situations.

drought
A prolonged period without success.

dynasty
A team that has an extended period of success, usually winning multiple championships in the process.

established
Showed to be legitimate.

journeyman
A player who has played for many teams or has been unable to find a specific role.

nautical
Concerning sailors and navigating on the water.

polished
Accomplished and skillful.

silky
Suave and smooth.

swingman
A player who can play both guard and forward.

tenacious
Persistent, determined.

INDEX